For my brother David for all the hours
we spent together as kids finding bugs.

BACKYARD BUGS

Helen Milroy

FREMANTLE PRESS

I watch an **ant**

march

up the tree

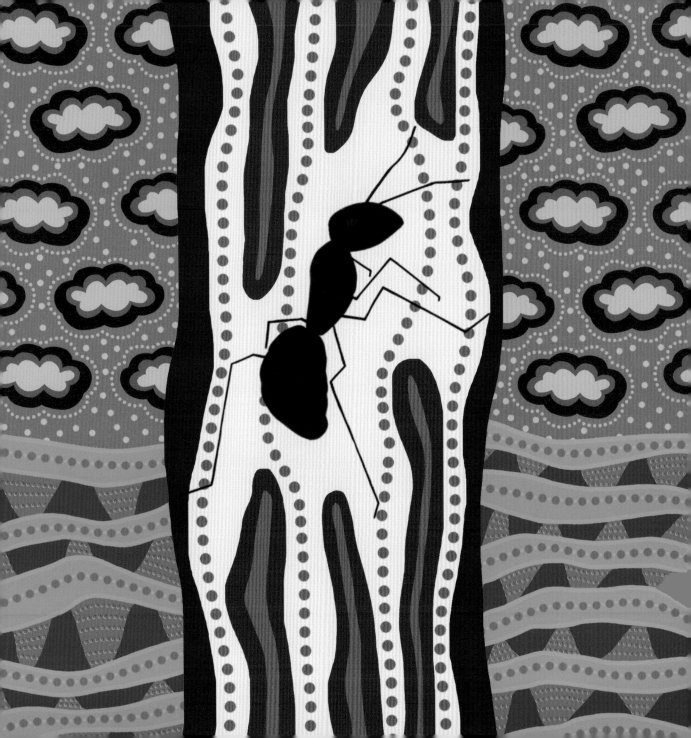

while dragonfly
flits
close to me

the earthworm

((wriggles))

in the sand

as beetle

trips

across the land

a cricket

chirps

his happy song

and honey-bee
buz, buz, buzzzZes
along

caterpillar

turns into

butterfly

while spider

hangs

against the sky

snail and slug

slip slide

on leaves

then **ladybird**
lands
upon my sleeve!

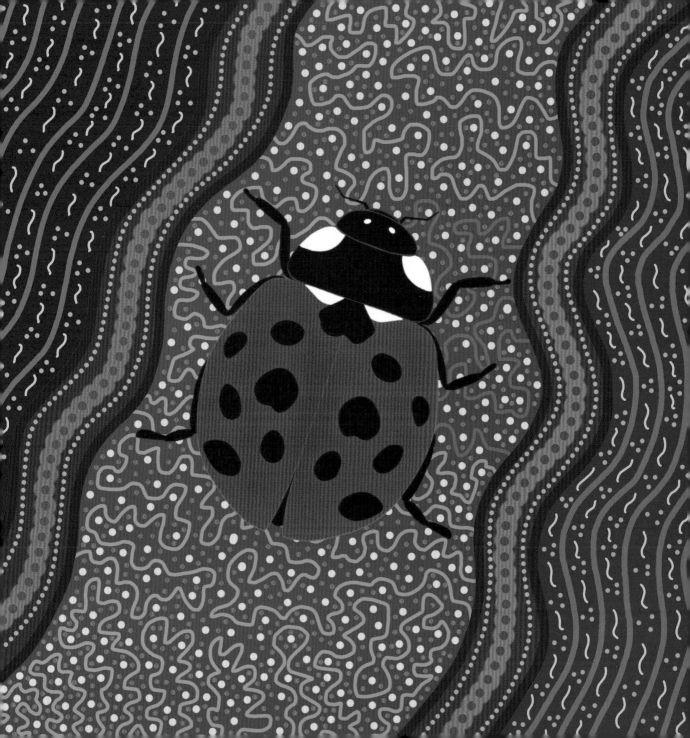

In my backyard
there's lots to see.

I love the bugs
that live near me!

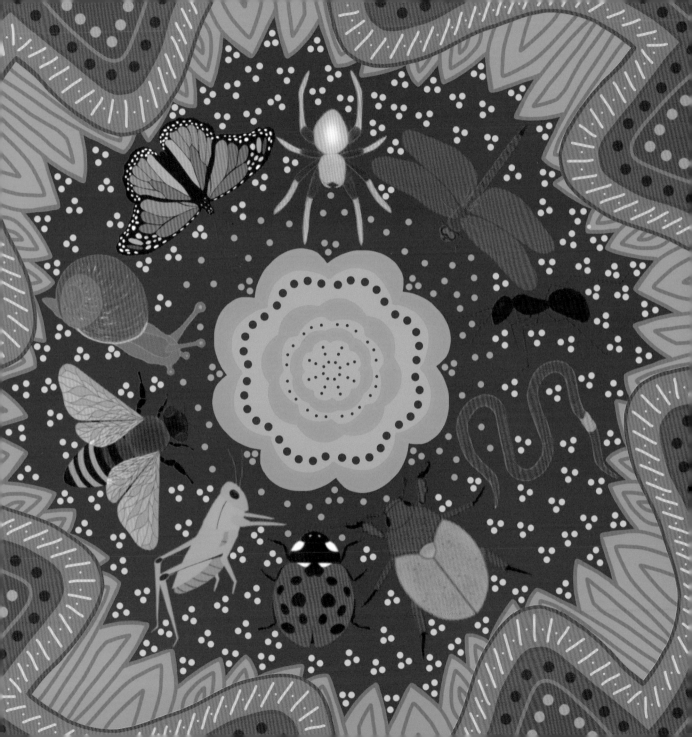

Helen Milroy is a descendant of the Palyku people of the Pilbara region of Western Australia. She was born and educated in Perth. Helen has always had a passionate interest in health and wellbeing, especially for children. Helen studied medicine at the University of Western Australia. She is currently a professor at UWA, Consultant Child and Adolescent Psychiatrist, and Commissioner with the National Mental Health Commission. Helen was recently appointed as the AFL's first Indigenous Commissioner.

First published 2021 by
FREMANTLE PRESS

Fremantle Press Inc. trading as Fremantle Press
25 Quarry Street, Fremantle WA 6160
www.fremantlepress.com.au

Illustration medium: freehand digital artwork.
Designed by Rebecca Mills.
Printed by Everbest Investment Printing Limited, China.

ISBN: 9781760990282.

Fremantle Press is supported by the State Government through
the Department of Local Government, Sport and Cultural Industries.